D0457379

Francine Poulet
Meets the
Ghost Raccoon

Tales from Deckawoo Drive

Volume Two

Francine Poulet Meets the Ghost Raccoon

Kate DiCamillo

illustrated by Chris Van Dusen

CANDLEWICK PRESS

Text copyright © 2015 by Kate DiCamillo
Illustrations copyright © 2015 by Chris Van Dusen

First edition 2015

Library of Congress Catalog Card Number 2014951801
ISBN 978-0-7636-6886-0

15 16 17 18 19 20 BVG 10 9 8 7 6 5 4 3 2 1

Printed in Berryville, VA, U.S.A.

This book was typeset in Mrs. Eaves.
The illustrations were done in gouache.

Candlewick Press
99 Dover Street
Somerville, Massachusetts 02144

visit us at www.candlewick.com

For Lisa Beck, who is good in every crisis
K. D.

To my friends Dave and Terri, with love
C. V.

Chapter One

Francine Poulet was an animal control officer.

She hailed from a long line of animal control officers.

Francine's father, Clement Poulet, had been an animal control officer, and Francine's grandmother Nanette Poulet had been an animal control officer, too.

Francine had won many animal control trophies—forty-seven of them, to be exact.

In addition, Francine was the Gizzford County record holder for most animals controlled. She had successfully and officially and expeditiously (for the most part) captured dogs, cats, rats, pigs, snakes, squirrels, chipmunks, bats, raccoons, and, also, fish.

One time, Francine had faced down a bear. The bear and Francine had stared at each other for a long time.

The bear blinked first.

Francine Poulet was an excellent animal control officer.

She was never, ever afraid.

Late one afternoon in May, the phone at the Animal Control Center rang.

Francine Poulet was sitting at her desk. She answered the phone. She said, "Animal Control Officer Francine Poulet here. How may I help you?"

"Yes, hello," said the voice at the other end. "Mrs. Bissinger speaking."

"Uh-huh," said Francine.

"I am being tormented," said Mrs. Bissinger.

"Yep," said Francine.

Everyone who called the Animal Control Center was being tormented in one way or another. Francine was never surprised to hear about it.

Nothing frightened Francine Poulet, and nothing surprised her either.

"A most unusual raccoon has come to reside on my roof," said Mrs. Bissinger.

4

"Right," said Francine. "Raccoon on the roof. What's your address?"

"Perhaps you were not listening," said Mrs. Bissinger. "This is not your average raccoon."

"Right," said Francine, "not your average raccoon." She leaned back in her chair. And then she leaned back a bit farther.

Francine leaned back so far that the front legs of the chair lifted off the ground. This was a bad habit of Francine's. Her father, Clement Poulet, had tried to break her of it, but he had never succeeded.

"One of these days, Franny," her father used to say, "you are going to tip all the way backwards in that chair and whack your head, and then you will be sorry."

Clement Poulet was dead, and it been many years since he had warned his daughter about chair-tipping. Francine missed Clement. She even missed his dire predictions. However, she had yet to tip all the way backward and whack her head. Francine had been gifted with an extraordinary sense of balance.

"This raccoon," said Mrs. Bissinger, "shimmers."

"He what?" said Francine.

"Shimmers," said Mrs. Bissinger. "He seems to glow. In addition, and more disturbingly, this raccoon calls my name."

Francine slowly lowered the chair legs to the floor.

"Interesting," said Francine. "The raccoon says, 'Mrs. Bissinger'?"

"No," said Mrs. Bissinger. "He says 'Tammy.' He screams my first name. He screams it like a banshee. Perhaps this raccoon is a ghost raccoon?"

"There are no ghosts," said Francine Poulet. "And there are no ghosts of raccoons."

"Be that as it may," said Mrs. Bissinger, "there is a shimmery raccoon on my roof who calls my name. And so on."

"Right," said Francine. "The address?"

"Forty-two fourteen Fleeker Street," said Mrs. Bissinger.

"I'll see you tonight," said Francine.

"Bring a ladder," said Mrs. Bissinger. "The roof is very steep and very high. You are not afraid of heights, are you?"

"I am not afraid of anything," said Francine.

"How inspiring," said Mrs. Bissinger. "I look forward to making your acquaintance."

"And I look forward to catching your raccoon," said Francine. She hung up the phone. She leaned back in her chair and studied her trophies, all forty-seven of them. She started to hum.

Francine's father had always told her that she was like a refrigerator.

What he said exactly was, "Franny, you are the genuine article. You are solid.

You are certain. You are like a refrigerator. You hum."

Francine leaned back in her chair. She balanced the chair on two legs.

"A talking ghost raccoon?" she said. "I don't think so."

She hummed louder. She leaned back farther.

"Watch out, Mr. Raccoon," said Francine Poulet. "I am going to get you."

Chapter Two

That night, Francine Poulet drove her animal control truck to 4214 Fleeker Street. She rang the doorbell.

A woman wearing a large diamond necklace, dangly ruby earrings, several flashy rings, and a multi-stone brooch answered the door.

Francine squinted.

"Mrs. Bissinger?" she said.

"Exactly," said Mrs. Bissinger. "Tammy Bissinger. How do you do?"

"I do just fine," said Francine. "I am here about your raccoon."

"I assumed," said Mrs. Bissinger. She stood there glittering. "And so on," she said.

"Well," said Francine, "okay, then. I think I will just head up on the roof and catch this raccoon."

"You will find him to be a wily adversary, almost supernatural in his abilities," said Mrs. Bissinger.

"Uh-huh," said Francine.

"He insists on saying my name," said Mrs. Bissinger.

"Yep," said Francine. "You told me that."

"Has a raccoon ever said your name?"

"Nope," said Francine. She turned her back on Mrs. Bissinger and headed to the truck.

She unloaded her ladder. She retrieved her net. She checked her flashlight for batteries. And then Francine put the ladder

13

against the side of the house. She turned the flashlight on and put it between her teeth. She grasped the net firmly in one hand and a rung of the ladder firmly in the other.

Francine Poulet started to climb.

As she climbed, she hummed.

She was solid. She was certain. She was Animal Control Officer Francine Poulet.

At the top of the ladder, Francine stepped out onto the roof. She took the flashlight out of her mouth. She turned and shone it back on the ground, and there was Mrs. Bissinger, standing and looking up at her, all her jewelry twinkling and glowing.

"Be careful!" shouted Mrs. Bissinger. "He is an extraordinary raccoon! He shimmers! He screams like a banshee! And so on!"

"Right," said Francine. "Yep. Yep. You told me. He shimmers. He screams like a banshee. Got it."

Francine turned off the flashlight.

The thing about catching wild animals is not to let them smell your fear.

Since Francine Poulet was never, ever afraid, this was not a problem for her.

The other thing about catching wild animals is that the more you chase them, the faster they run.

It is best to let the wild ones come to you.

Francine sat down on the roof. She stretched her arms and legs. She cracked her knuckles. She hummed.

"What are you doing?" shouted Mrs. Bissinger from down below.

Francine ignored her.

It was pleasant, sitting on the roof in the dark, ignoring Mrs. Bissinger.

Francine hummed louder.

"Oh, Mr. Raccoon," whispered Francine, "everything is perfectly fine. There is no one here except for you and me, and we are friendly friends, you and me."

Francine closed her eyes. She hummed some more.

She heard a footfall. And then another footfall.

Francine smiled a very big smile without opening her eyes. She kept humming. Slowly, slowly she reached out and put her hand on the animal control net.

And then there came a high-pitched scream.

It did not sound like the raccoon was saying "Tammy."

Instead, it sounded like this: *"Frannnnnnnnnnnyyyyyy!"*

Francine couldn't believe it. The raccoon was saying her name.

She opened her eyes just in time to see a shimmery, raccoon-shaped object flying through the air. It was headed directly for her.

"Frannnnnnnnnyyyyyyyyyy!" screamed the ghost raccoon.

Animal Control Officer Francine
Poulet, daughter of Animal Control Officer Clement Poulet, granddaughter of
Animal Control Officer Nanette Poulet,
was, for the first time in her life, afraid.

In fact, she was terrified.

Chapter Three

The raccoon was running straight toward Francine. His teeth were bared, and they did not look like ghost teeth. They looked like raccoon teeth.

"Frannnnnnnnnnyyyyyyyyyy!" screamed the raccoon.

Francine Poulet dropped her net. "Aaaaack!" she screamed back.

Francine's heart was beating so fast that she thought it might actually leap out of her chest and skitter across the roof.

She started to run.

She could feel the raccoon at her heels. She could smell his breath, and it did not smell good.

Where was the ladder? Where had she left it? She couldn't think.

"Frannnnnnyyyyyyyyyyyyy!" screamed the raccoon.

No one in Francine's life had ever called her "Franny" except for her father.

How did the raccoon know to call her secret name?

Was the raccoon truly a ghost?

These were exactly the kinds of questions that Francine did not think she should be considering at this juncture.

She looked around her wildly. She spotted the ladder. She ran toward it. She had one foot on the ladder and one on the roof when she heard Mrs. Bissinger's disembodied voice say, "Have you captured the raccoon?"

"What?" shouted Francine.

"Frannnnnnnyyyyyyyyyyyy!" screamed the raccoon.

"The raccoon," said Mrs. Bissinger. "Have you captured him?"

"Forget the raccoon," said Francine. "I am trying to save my life here."

"How disappointing," said Mrs. Bissinger. "And so on."

Francine started to climb down the ladder.

"I told you he was *not* an ordinary raccoon," said Mrs. Bissinger's extremely annoying voice. There was a long pause. Mrs. Bissinger cleared her throat. "But then, I had heard that you were not an ordinary animal control officer."

Something about this comment stopped Francine. Mrs. Bissinger was right. Francine Poulet was not an ordinary animal control officer. She was the owner of forty-seven trophies. She was the proud holder of the Gizzford County record for most animals controlled. What was she doing running from a raccoon just because he was screaming "Frannnnnnnnnyyyyyyyyyyyy"?

Francine started to climb back up the ladder.

"How inspiring," said Mrs. Bissinger. "How truly inspiring. Back into battle. And so on."

Francine got to the top of the ladder. She put one foot on the roof and then the other foot. She crouched. She waited. Everything was very silent. Francine could hear her heart beating. She was afraid. She knew that it was dangerous to be afraid. But she wasn't sure how, exactly, to *stop* being afraid.

"Mr. Raccoon?" whispered Francine.

The raccoon answered her. He answered her by screaming his terrible scream and by bounding out of the darkness and throwing himself directly at her.

The raccoon hit Francine with such tremendous, raccoon-y force that she lost her balance and fell forward.

"Oooof," said Francine.

Not knowing what else to do, she grabbed hold of the raccoon. She wrapped her arms around him.

He didn't *feel* like a ghost. He felt extremely solid. He smelled like a dirty winter coat.

Also, he was very loud.

He kept screaming.

Actually, there was a lot of screaming. Someone else was screaming, too. Who was it?

It was Francine Poulet who was
screaming!

How embarrassing, thought Francine.

But still, she couldn't seem to stop.

She and the raccoon were rolling
around together and they were both
screaming, and then, somehow, she and
the raccoon were falling.

They were falling together, and they were falling for what seemed like a very long time.

Francine thought, *Mrs. Bissinger is right. This is a very tall roof.*

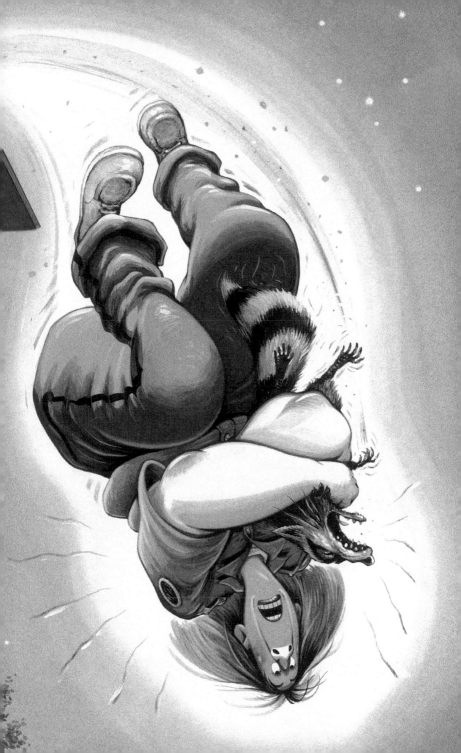

And then Animal Control Officer Francine Poulet hit the ground.

Everything went dark.

Chapter Four

Francine Poulet woke up in a hospital bed. Her left leg was in a cast, and her right arm was in a cast. Her neck was in a brace. Her head hurt.

"I am solid as a refrigerator," said Francine out loud.

These words didn't sound very believable.

"I am Animal Control Officer Francine Poulet," said Francine.

These words didn't sound very believable either.

She sniffed. She smelled cigar smoke.

"Over here, Franny," she heard someone say.

Francine turned her head very, very slowly and saw that her father was standing beside her bed.

"Pop?" she said.

"The one and only," said Clement Poulet.

"Aren't you dead?" said Francine.

"Absolutely," said her father.

"Oh," said Francine.

Clement Poulet puffed on his cigar. He blew the smoke into the air above Francine's bed.

"What were you doing up there, Franny?" he said.

"Up where?" said Francine.

"Up on the roof," said Clement Poulet.

"I was trying to catch that raccoon," said Francine.

"You panicked, though, didn't you?" said her father.

"I thought that raccoon knew my name. I thought that maybe the raccoon was a ghost."

"Pooh," said Clement Poulet, "that raccoon was nothing but a screamer. There aren't ghost raccoons, Franny. You know that."

Francine nodded, even though it hurt her head to nod. She knew there were no ghost raccoons. Of course she knew that.

"Also," said Clement Poulet, "Poulets do not panic. Even in the face of screaming raccoons."

Francine nodded. She knew that, too.

"It will be okay, Franny," said Clement Poulet.

"Will it?" she said. She felt a single tear roll out of her left eye and down her cheek. Francine missed her father telling her that everything was going to be okay. A tear rolled out of her right eye. And then tears fell from both eyes. Francine gave herself over to crying. After a while, she fell asleep.

When she woke up, her father was gone and Mrs. Bissinger was sitting in a chair beside the bed. She was wearing all her jewelry and she was holding a copy of the

Gizzford Gazette. The front-page headline read:

Below the headline, there was a picture of Francine Poulet taken at the previous year's awards banquet. She was holding a trophy (number 47) and smiling a very large smile.

Underneath the picture were the words "Raccoon Still at Large; Animal Control Officer Poulet Recuperating at the Gizzford Regional Hospital."

"They call that a tumble?" said Francine. "I fell three stories."

"Oh, good," said Mrs. Bissinger, "you're awake. Shall I read you the entire article?"

"No," said Francine. Her left foot, the one in the cast, itched.

"Can you scratch my left foot?" she said to Mrs. Bissinger.

Mrs. Bissinger put down the paper and stood up and gave Francine's foot a tentative little tap.

"How's that?" she said.

"That didn't help at all," said Francine.

"Oh, well," said Mrs. Bissinger. "I've never been much good at scratching people's feet." She picked up the paper and sat back down.

"It says here that your father was an animal control officer," said Mrs. Bissinger from behind the paper.

"That's true," said Francine.

"It says here," said Mrs. Bissinger, "that you are the most decorated animal control officer in the history of Gizzford."

"That's true, too," said Francine.

Mrs. Bissinger lowered the paper. She looked Francine in the eye. She said, "Yet you failed to capture my raccoon."

"Yes," said Francine. "I failed. I panicked." She turned her head and looked out the window. It was dark outside. Francine could see the lights of Gizzford winking and blinking, mocking her.

"Well," said Mrs. Bissinger, "your leg will heal and your arm will heal and you will exit the hospital and you will continue in the world. You will find a way to continue in spite of your failure, I suppose. And so on."

"No," said Francine.

"Beg pardon?" said Mrs. Bissinger.

"No," said Francine. "There will be no 'and so on.' I quit."

"What?" said Mrs. Bissinger.

"I quit," said Francine. "I am no longer Animal Control Officer Francine Poulet."

Chapter Five

Time passed.

First the cast came off Francine's arm, and then the cast came off her leg. Francine walked with a limp and a cane. Sometimes her leg ached. Sometimes her arm ached.

But she was healed, sort of.

And so, early one morning in September, Francine walked into the Animal Control Center and turned in her uniform.

"What is the meaning of this?" said Mordus Toopher, chairman of the board of the Animal Control Center.

Mordus Toopher wore a brown corduroy suit and a brown-and-orange toupee. The toupee had always disturbed Francine. It reminded her of a chipmunk pelt.

"I quit," said Francine.

"What are you saying to me?" said Mordus. He adjusted his chipmunk toupee.

"I'm saying I quit," said Francine.

"You have battled many a snake and outwitted many a squirrel," said Mordus. "You have stared a bear, that dark and ferocious mystery, in the eye, and that dark and ferocious mystery blinked first."

"True," said Francine.

"And now you have reached this impasse of the soul, this gloomy, doomy time of self-appraisal. I wonder: Will you dwell here in your small shame and sad defeat? Will you truly allow yourself to be undone by one ignoble screaming raccoon?"

"Yes," said Francine.

Mordus Toopher shook his head. His toupee slipped a little. "Unbelievable," he said. He shook his head again. He righted his toupee.

"I am deeply saddened," he said. "Deeply saddened, yes. It is the end of an era. It is the end of an era that began with Nanette Poulet and continued with Clement Poulet and now it ends; it ends. The era ends with a dull, inharmonious thud. It ends with Francine and a raccoon."

"Can I have my trophies?" said Francine.

"I am afraid that the trophies must remain here," said Mordus, "property of Gizzford Animal Control Center, procured under the auspices, et cetera, et cetera. And et cetera." He smiled a sad smile.

"Right," said Francine. "Okay. Well, thanks for all the good times."

Mordus Toopher raised his right hand and waved good-bye. "The end of an era," he said. "The end."

Francine Poulet walked out of the Animal Control Center. She did not look back.

♦ ♦ ♦

But that evening, Francine limped down to Fleeker Street and hid in a rhododendron bush. She studied Mrs. Bissinger's house.

She watched the dusk turn into a velvety darkness. She watched as a gibbous moon rose in the sky and shone on Mrs. Bissinger's empty, extremely tall, extremely steep roof.

There was no raccoon in sight.

"You weren't even a ghost," said Francine to the empty roof. "You were just a raccoon. I panicked. And Poulets never panic."

"Why are you hiding in my rhododendron?" said a voice.

Francine looked up. Mrs. Bissinger was standing above her, bejeweled and gleaming.

"I am not hiding," said Francine. "And so on."

"And so on," agreed Mrs. Bissinger. She sighed. She twinkled. "It is time to move on, Francine. The raccoon is gone. You must go, too."

"Okay," said Francine.

Mrs. Bissinger walked away. Francine continued to crouch in the rhododendron bush. She looked away from the roof, up into the dark sky. She could see some stars, but not many. Shouldn't there be more stars? The world seemed very dark.

Her arm ached. And her heart. Francine's heart ached, too.

She didn't know who she was. She was not an animal control officer. And she was not a Poulet, because Poulets never panic.

"Who am I?" said Francine to the dark sky.

There was no answer.

"Tell me who I am!" shouted Francine.

And then, from somewhere far away, there came an answer.

"Go home, Francine!"

Francine looked up. Mrs. Bissinger was standing in a lighted window. "Go home!" she shouted again. She waved her arms around.

Francine stood up. She exited the rhododendron bush. She went home.

Chapter Six

Francine Poulet got a job as a cashier at Clyde's Bait, Feed, Tackle, and Animal Necessities.

Her left leg, the one she had broken when she fell from Mrs. Bissinger's roof with the raccoon in her arms, continued to ache. So Francine sat on a stool as she rang up dog chow and plastic worms, chicken feed and rawhide bones, fishing poles and horse bridles.

For some reason, Clyde's Bait, Feed, Tackle, and Animal Necessities was bedeviled by flies. Francine kept a fly swatter on hand at all times. She got very good at whacking flies.

Other than the flies, it was a quiet existence.

There were no emergency calls. There were no dramatic chases. There were no raccoons who called her name. There was no Mrs. Bissinger. And so on.

Clement Poulet did not show up in the brightly lit aisles of Clyde's. There was no smell of cigar smoke. There was no suggestion that Francine was disappointing anyone or that she was not as solid as a refrigerator.

Also, a stool was not a chair. It was very, very hard to tip backward on the legs of a stool. Francine did not even try. It seemed too dangerous.

Francine sat. The days passed.

She rang up a lot of dog chow.

She killed a lot of flies. In fact, she kept a running tally of how many flies she had whacked, just so she could convince herself that she was making progress of some sort.

On the day that Francine killed her 238th fly, a girl and a boy came into Clyde's Bait, Feed, Tackle, and Animal Necessities.

The girl said, "Where are your sweets?"

"We don't deal in sweets," said Francine Poulet.

She could hear Fly 239 buzzing at her ear.

"Not even licorice?" said the girl.

"No licorice," said Francine.

Fly 239 zoomed back and forth in front of her, taunting her.

"Hey," said the boy, "I know you."

Francine took her eyes off the fly and looked at the boy.

"My name is Frank," he said.

"Good for you," said Francine.

"And you are Animal Control Officer Francine Poulet," said Frank. "Once you were on official business on our street. Also, I saw your picture in the paper."

"What about cough drops?" said the girl. "Do you have cough drops? Sometimes when a store doesn't sell candy, they will sell cough drops."

"Stella," said Frank, "there aren't any sweets here."

"That just doesn't seem right to me," said Stella. "That seems wrong. How can you run a store without selling sweets?"

"You are a highly decorated animal control officer," said Frank to Francine. "You are from a long line of animal control officers."

Francine's toes felt funny. Her stomach was squiffy.

"Why are you working here?" said Frank.

"That's none of your beeswax," said Francine. She swung the fly swatter through the air in a menacing sort of way, even though Fly 239 had disappeared.

"You fell off a roof with a raccoon in your arms," said Frank. "You took a tumble."

"It was not a tumble," said Francine. "It was way more than a tumble."

"I read about it in the paper," said Frank.

"Frank reads the whole paper. He reads it from back to front," said Stella. "He reads every word of it, and he remembers it all. That's what Frank does. That's the way he is."

"I pay attention," said Frank.

"He worries," said Stella.

"The raccoon got away," said Frank. "And the raccoon that got away is a screamer."

Francine's toes twitched. Her heart thumped.

Clement Poulet had called the raccoon a screamer, too.

"So?" said Francine. "So what?"

"So, I know where your screaming raccoon is," said Frank.

Chapter Seven

"He is not my raccoon," said Francine.

"He is on the roof of the Lincoln Sisters' house. I have heard him and I have seen him. I have watched him through my binoculars. I own a very good pair of binoculars."

"Good for you, kid," said Francine Poulet.

"I keep an eye and an ear on things on Deckawoo Drive," said Frank.

"He worries," said Stella.

"Deckawoo Drive?" said Francine. "I once caught a pig on Deckawoo Drive."

"That's Mercy Watson!" said Stella. "She likes to eat toast with a great deal of butter on it."

"Raccoons carry rabies," said Frank. "Raccoons bite. Raccoons steal things. I read an article about a raccoon who stole a baby right out of its cradle."

"What?" said Stella.

"It's true," said Frank.

"What was the baby's name?" said Stella.

"That is an unimportant detail," said Frank. "The important thing is that it happened. Raccoons are dangerous."

Francine felt her toes curling up. Her arm ached. Her leg ached. Fly 239 flew by. Francine looked down at her hands. They were shaking.

"You're afraid," said Frank.

"I am not afraid," said Francine.

"Yes, you are," said Frank. "Your hands are shaking. That is a sign of fear."

"I'm not well," said Francine. "I don't feel good."

"You're never going to feel good until you face that raccoon," said Frank.

"Get out of here, kid," said Francine. She swung her fly swatter in the direction of the door.

"What would your father say?" said Frank.

"What?" said Francine. She felt her heart skitter and stutter inside of her.

"Your father. Animal Control Officer Clement Poulet."

"You didn't know my father," said Francine.

"No," said Frank. "I did not. But I read about him. He was a very brave man, and in the article in the paper, it said that he was proud of you."

Francine stared at Frank.

Frank stared at Francine.

Stella sighed a deep sigh. "You know what I wish? I wish we could go someplace where they sell sweets. I wish we could go to a place where they sell jelly beans or chocolate-covered peanuts or gumdrops. I love gumdrops."

"You were an outstanding animal control officer once," said Frank.

"I was," said Francine. "I was one of the greats. And then I panicked. Poulets do not panic." She stared down at the fly swatter in her trembling hands.

"Maybe you are still a great animal control officer," said Frank. "Why don't you find out? Come to Deckawoo Drive and help us capture the raccoon."

Frank took hold of Stella's hand. "Come on, Stella," he said. "We'll go and get you some sweets."

Frank and Stella left Clyde's Bait, Feed, Tackle, and Animal Necessities.

Francine sat on her stool. Fly 239 buzzed around her head. A great shaft of sunlight came in through the plate-glass windows of Clyde's and made the bags of dog chow glow like misshapen ghosts.

Frank's words echoed in Francine's head. *Maybe you are still a great animal control officer.*

Maybe.

Could it be true?

♦ ♦ ♦

The door to Clyde's opened, and Stella walked in.

"Close your eyes and hold out your hand," said Stella.

Francine Poulet closed her eyes and held out her hand. She felt a small tickle in the center of her palm.

"Okay," said Stella. "You can look now."

Francine looked down. In her hand was a gumdrop, a green one.

"You should come and get the raccoon," said Stella. "It would make Frank happy. He worries."

After Stella left Clyde's Bait, Feed, Tackle, and Animal Necessities, Francine put the gumdrop in her mouth. It tasted sweet.

Francine rocked her stool back and forth. She felt one leg of it lift the tiniest bit off the floor.

And Francine Poulet made a small noise that sounded almost like a hum.

Chapter Eight

Former Animal Control Officer Francine Poulet stood in the darkness on Deckawoo Drive.

She held a net. Her hands were trembling. The net was moving up and down and swaying back and forth.

Frank was standing at Francine's side.

"Shhhhh," said Frank.

"I didn't say anything," said Francine. The net bounced up and down.

Frank handed Francine the binoculars.

"Look," he said. "Is that your raccoon?"

Francine put the net on the ground. She took the binoculars. She held them up and looked through them. She saw the raccoon sitting on the roof, staring at her.

The moon was bright, and it was shining on the raccoon's fur. The raccoon shimmered.

"Eeep," said Francine.

"What?" said Frank.

"That is the raccoon," said Francine. "That is him. He is that. Oh, oh, oh. Whoop. Eep."

"Calm down," said Frank.

"I'm afraid," said Francine.

Frank took hold of her hand.

"That doesn't help," said Francine.

Frank squeezed her hand very hard. "Okay," said Francine. "Maybe it helps a little."

"This is the plan, Miss Poulet," said Frank. "I will hold the ladder. And you will climb up it, and you will take your net with you. You will capture the raccoon with your net, just as you have captured other raccoons with your net. Remember, you have forty-seven trophies."

"Forty-seven," said Francine in a voice of wonder.

"You got into a staring contest with a bear and you won," said Frank.

"I did?" said Francine.

"You did," said Frank. "Climb the ladder, Miss Poulet."

"Okay," said Francine. "I will climb now."

Francine grabbed hold of the ladder. She took a step up and then another step up. She tried to hum, but she couldn't remember how. Suddenly, humming seemed like a very complicated thing.

"Just climb," whispered Frank.

So Francine climbed. She climbed some more.

And suddenly, there she was, standing on the roof, her whole body trembling like a tiny leaf in a ferocious November wind.

From somewhere on the roof, the raccoon screamed.

"Miss Poulet?" said Frank.

"Yes?" said Francine.

"Be brave," said Frank.

"Okay," said Francine. She sat down. She put her head between her knees.

"Miss Poulet?" said Frank. "Miss Poulet?"

And then from down below came another voice. The other voice said, "Franklin Endicott, I would like it very much if you explained yourself."

"There is a raccoon on your roof, Miss Lincoln," said Frank. "And I have arranged for the best animal control officer in the county, in the country, maybe even in the entire world, to catch your raccoon. That animal control officer is on your roof right now."

A door slammed. "Sister!" said a different voice. "Are you all right?"

"Most certainly not! Some strange woman is on our roof."

Francine raised her head from her knees. She peered over the edge of the roof. There were two old women in bathrobes staring up at her.

One of the women waved. She said, "Hello, my name is Baby. And this is my sister, Eugenia."

"We're not at a garden party, Baby," said Eugenia. "There is no need to introduce yourself."

"And who are you?" said Baby to Francine.

"Um," said Francine. Her stomach felt squiffy.

"Are you truly an animal control officer?" shouted Eugenia. "Or are you just some

81

nut job gallivanting on my roof? And more to the point, who says I have a raccoon on my roof to begin with?"

"Oh, but Sister," said Baby Lincoln, "we do have a raccoon living on our roof. I have seen him many times. And I have thought it would be wonderful if we could name him."

"Name him?" said Eugenia. "*Name* him?"

A door banged open. A woman shouted, "Frank? Eugenia? Baby? Is everything okay?"

"Hello, Mrs. Watson," said Frank. "Everything is fine. There is a raccoon on the Lincoln Sisters' roof, and we are in the process of capturing it."

"Are you sure it's a raccoon?" said Mrs. Watson. "It looks like a woman."

82

"That's Animal Control Officer Francine Poulet," said Frank.

"Oh," said Mrs. Watson. "Of course. I didn't recognize her in the dark. Hello, dear. You once helped us locate our porcine wonder. Hello."

And then, in the middle of this slightly inane exchange of pleasantries, there came a terrible, bloodcurdling scream.

"Frannnnnnnnnnnnnnnnnnnnnyyyyyyyyyyyyyyyyyyyy!"

Chapter Nine

Francine shivered. She trembled.

The raccoon screamed again.

"What a rude noise," said Eugenia.

"It is just the raccoon," said Baby. "He screams. Have you never heard him scream before, Sister?"

"No," said Eugenia. "I have never heard him scream before. I am too busy to listen for screaming raccoons."

"Frannnnnnnnnnnyyyyy!" screamed the raccoon.

"I think he is lonely!" said Baby.

"For heaven's sake, Baby," said Eugenia, "the raccoon is not lonely."

Francine's heart skittered and skipped and thumped. She stayed crouched on the roof.

"That animal control woman is worthless," said Eugenia. "She is doing absolutely nothing."

"I must say that she was very helpful when Mercy went missing," said Mrs. Watson.

"She looks like a fraud to me," said Eugenia.

"She is not a fraud," said Frank. "She is the genuine article."

The genuine article!

Those were the words that Francine's father had used. That was exactly what Clement Poulet had said: You are the genuine article, Franny.

"Raaaaaaaaaannnnnnyyyyyy!" screamed the raccoon.

Francine listened closely.

What was the raccoon saying?

"Grannnnnnnnnnnnnnnnnnnnnnnyyyy!" he screamed.

Why, he was saying absolutely nothing.

The raccoon did not know her name.

The raccoon was just screaming a scream. That was all.

Francine looked down at her hands on the net. They were not shaking. She was not trembling.

And why was that?

It was because she was the genuine article.

It was because she was as solid as a refrigerator.

It was because she was Francine Poulet.

Francine stood up.

"I am Animal Control Officer Francine Poulet!" she shouted. "I am the daughter of Animal Control Officer Clement Poulet and the granddaughter of Animal Control Officer Nanette Poulet."

"That's right," said Frank.

"Annnnnnnnnnnnnnnnnyyyyyyyy!" screamed the raccoon.

"I am the genuine article!" shouted Francine.

"Yes, you are," said Frank.

"What a lot of nonsense this is," said Eugenia. "Why don't you just do something?"

"I am now going to capture the raccoon!" shouted Francine.

88

"That is a really good idea, Miss Poulet," said Frank, "because the raccoon is standing right beside you."

Francine looked down.

Frank was exactly right. The raccoon was standing right beside her.

She looked at him. He looked at her. He bared his teeth. Francine bared her teeth back. She was not afraid. She was not one bit afraid.

Slowly, confidently, Francine raised the animal control net and lowered it over the raccoon.

Just like that.

"Kid?" said Francine.

"Yes, Miss Poulet?" said Frank.

"Get the cage ready, kid. I have captured the raccoon."

"I'm on it, Miss Poulet."

"I wonder if anyone is hungry," said Mrs. Watson from down below. "I wonder if I should make some toast."

And up on the roof, Francine Poulet started to hum.

Coda

Francine was reinstated by Mordus Toopher.

Mordus Toopher said, "This is a day of reclamation. This is a day when the shadows recede and the sun shines brightly. The true self is recalled and celebrated, and the trophies are returned to the animal control officer both literally and metaphorically. What I mean to say is: welcome back, Francine."

"Thank you, sir," said Francine. "I am happy to be back."

"And who is this young and earnest fellow?" said Mordus Toopher.

"My name is Franklin Endicott, sir," said Frank. "I am Miss Poulet's understudy. If you don't mind."

"Mind?" said Mordus Toopher. "How could I mind? Who would object to the passing on of such skill and knowledge? It is the beginning of an era. I applaud you."

"Me?" said Frank.

"Both of you," said Mordus Toopher. "I applaud both of you." He adjusted his toupee. "Happy, meaningful, and productive days are ahead, I'm sure."

◆ ◆ ◆

Francine and Frank rode together in the animal control truck.

Sometimes, in the purple light of early evening, Frank would say, "Remember when you were on that roof with the screaming raccoon and you forgot who you were, Miss Poulet?"

"Yes," said Francine.

"And then you remembered," said Frank.

"Yes," said Francine.

"It's good to know who you are," said Frank.

"I'm the genuine article, kid," said Francine. "And so are you. Now, let's concentrate. Let's keep our eyes open."

"My eyes are always open, Miss Poulet," said Frank.

"That's true," said Francine. "You're solid. You're certain. You hum, kid. You hum."

Kate DiCamillo is the renowned author of numerous books for young readers, including two Newbery Medal winners, *Flora & Ulysses: The Illuminated Adventures* and *The Tale of Despereaux,* as well as six books about Mercy Watson. She says, "Capable, fearless people like Francine Poulet have always fascinated me. I, alas, am not among their number. But hey, that's the beauty of being a writer—you get to imagine your way into other people's minds and hearts. You get to have them wrestle raccoons." Kate DiCamillo lives in Minneapolis.

Chris Van Dusen is the author-illustrator of *The Circus Ship, King Hugo's Huge Ego,* and *Randy Riley's Really Big Hit,* and the illustrator of all six books about Mercy Watson. He says, "Francine Poulet was one of my favorite characters from the original Mercy Watson series. I loved her strong, no-nonsense, take-charge persona. It's nice to see that she has a softer side, too, which Kate reveals so beautifully in this story." Chris Van Dusen lives in Maine.